Beo

wulf

Kim Smith was born in Billericay, Essex and now lives in a quiet hamlet near Ely, Cambridgeshire with her husband Cliff and three beautiful daughters.

Acknowledgements

Beowulf: Seamus Heaney
Beowulf text and translation: John Porter
The West Stow Anglo-Saxon Village, where the idea for the
book first came about.

Kim Smith

Beowulf

Pegasus

PEGASUS PAPERBACK

© Copyright 2013
Kim Smith

The right of Kim Smith to be identified as author of
this work has been asserted by her in accordance with the
Copyright, Designs and Patents Act 1988

A CIP catalogue record for this title is
available from the British Library

ISBN-978 1903490 808

Pegasus is an imprint of
Pegasus Elliot MacKenzie Publishers Ltd.
www.pegasuspublishers.com

First Published in 2013
Pegasus
Sheraton House Castle Park
Cambridge CB3 0AX England

Printed & Bound in Great Britain

Thank you to Sarah, Tina and Rodney for their input.

And,

My family for all their patience.

Introduction

Beowulf is a poem of more than 3000 lines long. It was written in England but tells a Scandinavian story, scribed somewhere roughly between 650AD and 1000AD. It has a dramatic narrative about a heroic warrior prince called Beowulf, whose untimely ending gives him immortal fame.

The English language has changed a lot since it was first written, and so it is read by those who study it as a translation.

My version is very condensed and more of a story than a poem; the emphasis being the illustrations. They are highly stylised as designed by the early Germanic tribes; the inspiration from historic stone carvings and jewellery and the monks with their manuscripts who came to Britain. The illustrations are painted in natural plant pigments onto linen; the most prominent are Weld-yellow, Woad-blue and Madder-red.

A rune, an early writing system was used by the Anglo-Saxons when they invaded the British Isles. The runes were engraved in stone, wood and metal. I have used these around the illustrations. A translation guide is available at the back of the book.

Illustrations

Inspiration for the illustrations is taken from the art known as knot work or interlacing, often referred to as Celtic Knot Work. I love the intricacy and challenge of the designs.

Knotwork represent the circle of life never ending: spirals mean the unfolding of life. Interlacing designs have their origins from the late Roman Empire. The Anglo-Saxons practiced and contributed to these by adding zoomorphic designs which include animals, plants or people.

The images have been painted on linen using natural pigments weld, woad, madder. These pigments would have been used by the Anglo-Saxons when dying their wool or linen for cloth. I have also used soot from my fireplace and elderberry pigment.

Beowulf

O, listen!

In days long, long ago a worthy and noble King ruled the Danes. His name was Scyld Scefing.

As a boy he grew up with nothing, found in a boat as a baby, but in time he became a strong and courageous King.

He was wise and loved by his people. Everybody listened when he spoke.

hen Scyld died, his people sent him adrift in a beautiful wooden boat, full of treasure.

His son Beow then became king. He had four grandchildren. One grandson, Hrothgar, became a great soldier and in time he became the ruler of Denmark.

While King he built a magnificent mead house called Heorot Hall, where there was plenty of merrymaking; songs, drinking of mead and feasting.

 here was one such feast with plenty of singing and dancing, a noisy affair.

The lyre, pipes and drums were so loud that it aroused a hideous monster. His name was Grendal. He ransacked the hall after dark, ripping apart the men as they slept and gorged on their bodies. Grendal continued his bloody campaign for twelve long years.

The merry making stopped.

The Danes prayed to their Gods. But the huge beast carried on. "Oh, what do we do?" They cried.

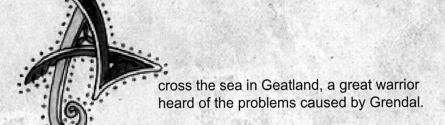cross the sea in Geatland, a great warrior heard of the problems caused by Grendal.

He sailed across in a beautiful curved wooden ship, with fourteen of his best soldiers, all dressed in their battle gear, each carrying shining silver swords, long spears of ash and round shields. Their helmets were decorated with boars and they wore heavy chainmail.

When they arrived they were challenged by a guard on horseback, "Who are you?"

"Beowulf is my name and we have come to help you."

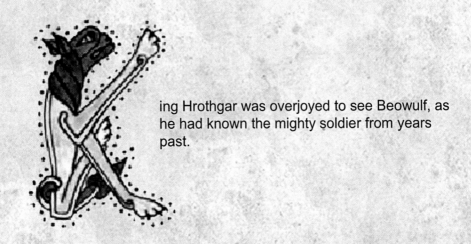 ing Hrothgar was overjoyed to see Beowulf, as he had known the mighty soldier from years past.

"But what can you do against such a demon?" asked the King.

Beowulf told King Hrothgar about how he fought with huge monsters and sea beasts. "I will fight Grendal without spear or sword, on equal terms!" he announced.

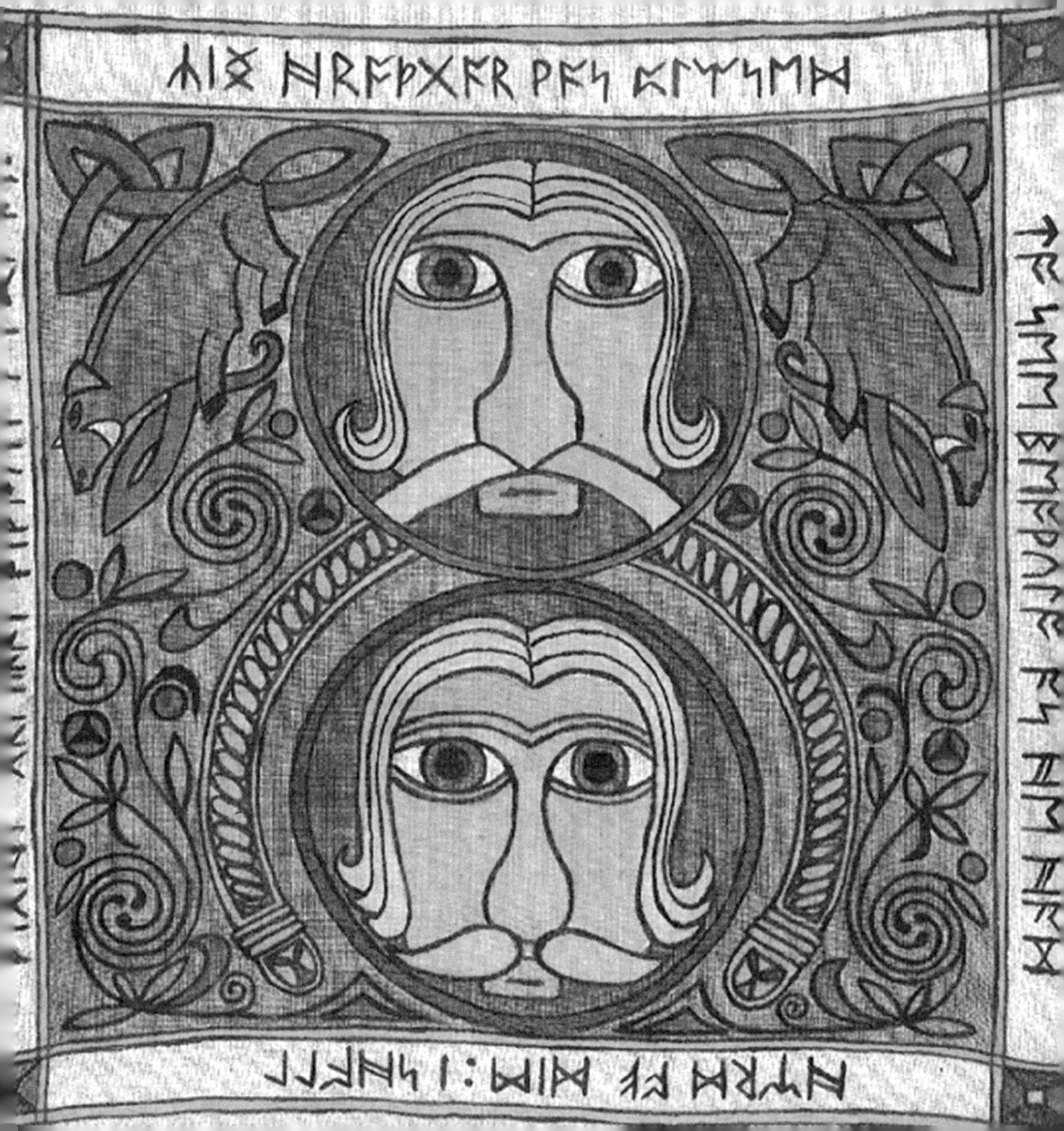

fter a splendid banquet, they all settled down to sleep.

Suddenly, Grendal burst in, furious at being disturbed by all the noise. He seized the first soldier, ripped him apart and sucked out all his blood and devoured his body. The mighty monster then reached for the mighty warrior Beowulf, but he was ready and grabbed the beast with his strong grip.

They fought, smashing benches and tables.

Grendal had found his match and could not escape.

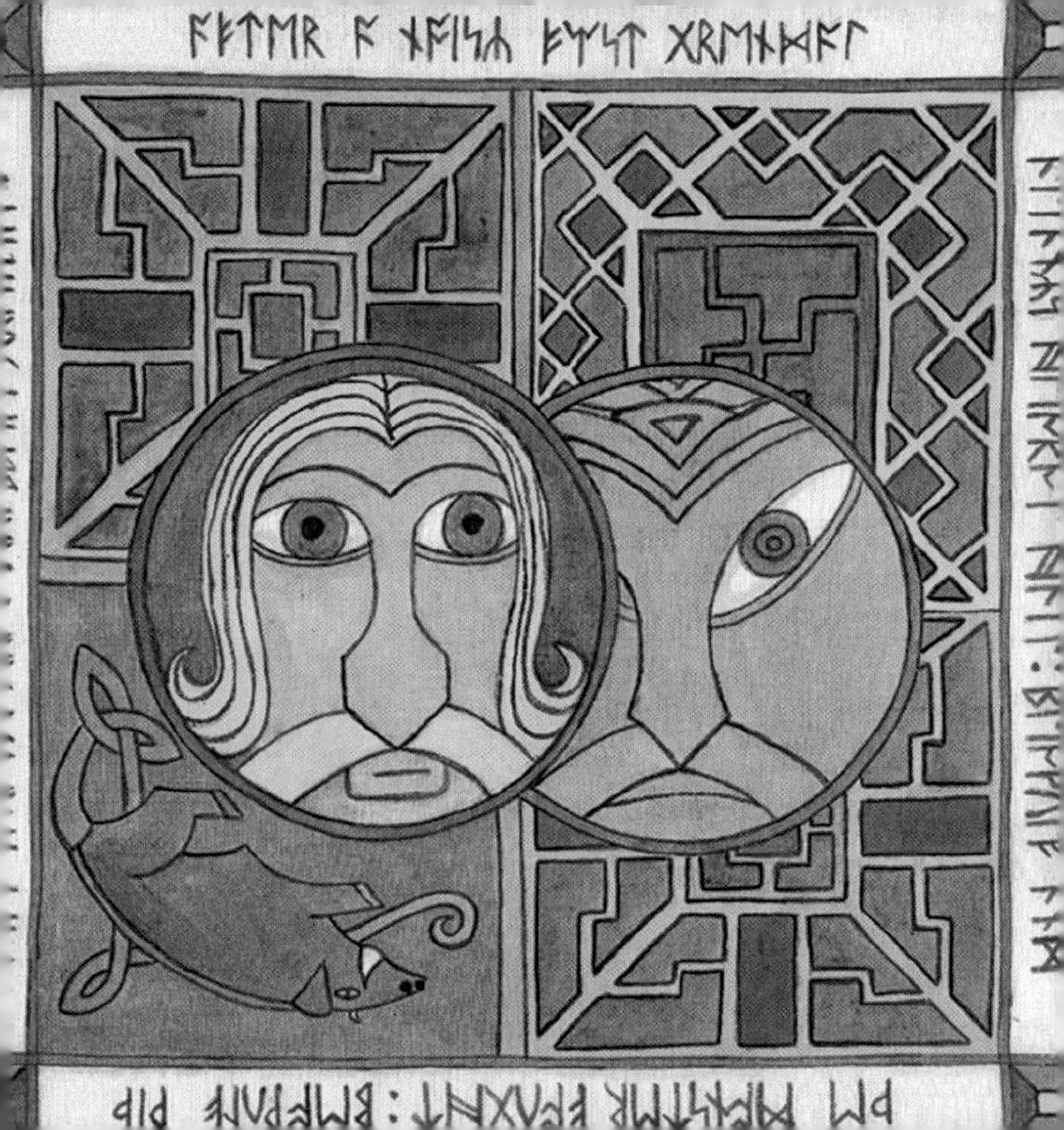

 HRRRRR!"

Grendal howled as his shoulder and arm was ripped from his immense body. He escaped, and galloped mortally wounded back to his deep, dark, and dismal cave, under a dank lake, where he died.

Beowulf triumphantly held up high, the bloodied limb for all to see.

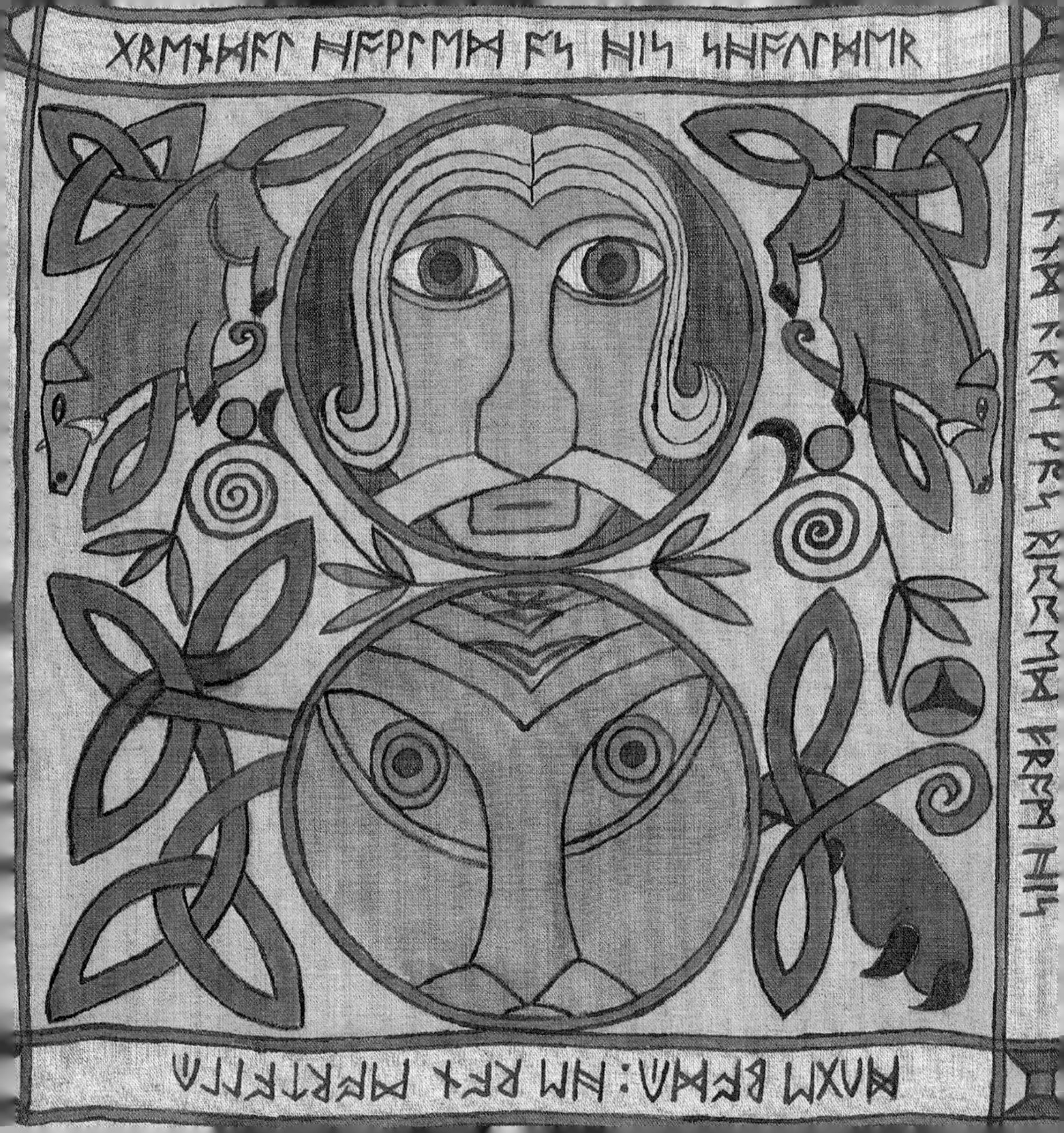

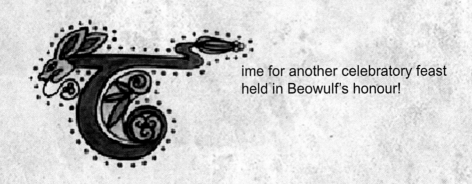ime for another celebratory feast held in Beowulf's honour!

Beowulf was given gifts, as were his soldiers.

Late into the night, as they all slept, an avenger crept slowly and menacingly into the hall.

It was Grendal's mother, who unhappy at the death of her son, grabbed a man with the strength of a warrior. She took him back to her lair at the bottom of the misty mere.

She took him back to her
lair at the bottom of the
misty mere.

On the way, she seized her son's weeping and bloodied arm that was hanging high up on a beam.

King Hrothgar was mortified, his comrade, Aeschere, had gone.

n the morning, King Hrothgar, together with Beowulf and his warriors, followed the tracks of Grendal's mother, to the deep dark, feted mere.

Beowulf swam deeply, killing sea beasts on the way, down to the squalled den where the fiendish beasts lived.

Grendal's mother was waiting...

They fought...

Using a sword called Hrunting, Beowulf slashed it against her flesh, without causing a scratch. Beowulf then grabbed an ancient sword. Swung it high, and with an almighty arc, cut off her head.

Grendal's mother was waiting...

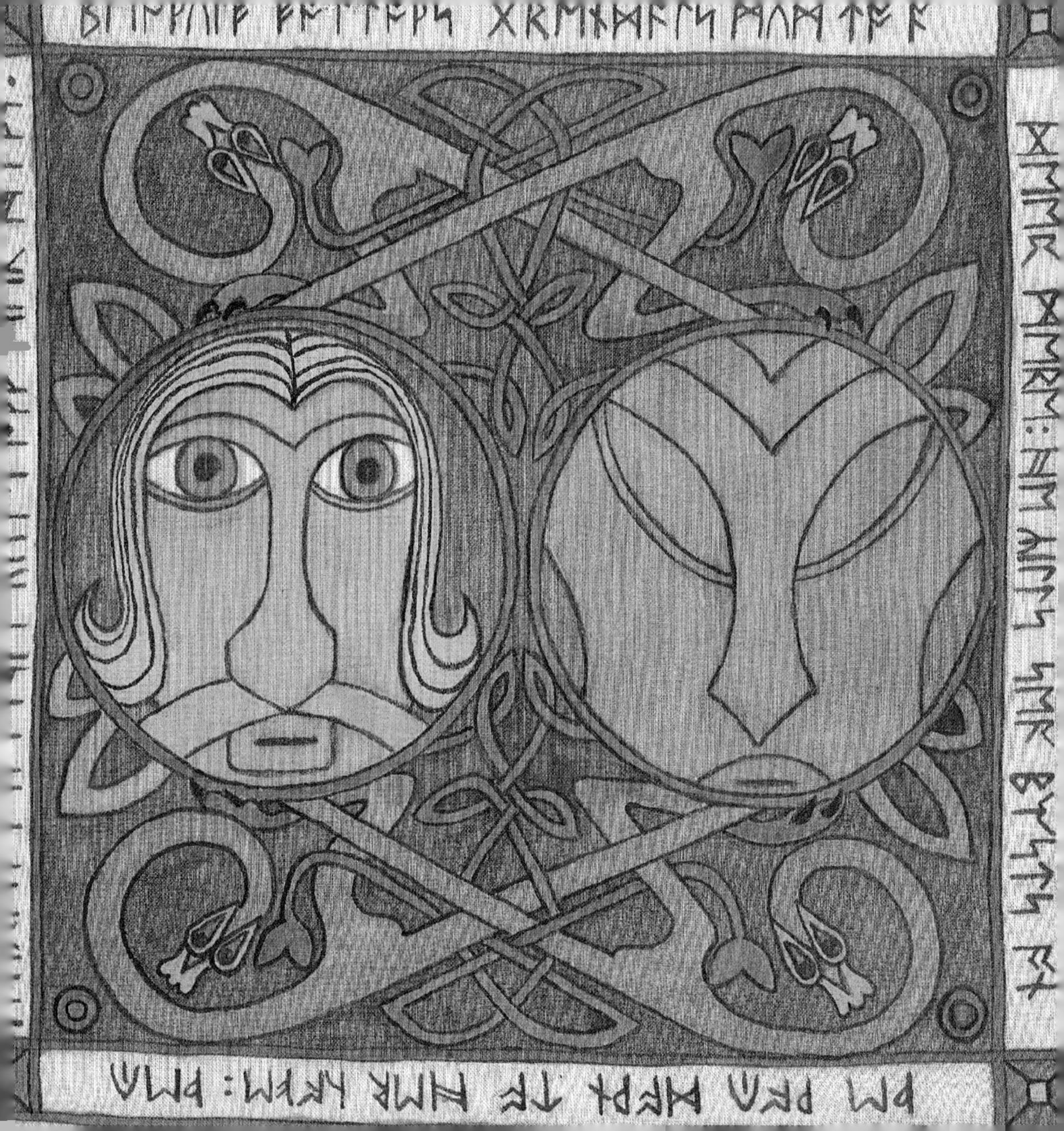

 et another magnificent feast was held in his honour!

More gifts were presented.

The next day, Beowulf and his men returned to the wooden long ship and sailed back to Sweden.

There, King Hygelac was told of the events concerning Grendal and his mother. As a thank you he gave Beowulf land and animals, with a hall of his own.

When the King died, Beowulf took his place.

And what a King he became, both powerful and good.

And what a King he became, both powerful and good.

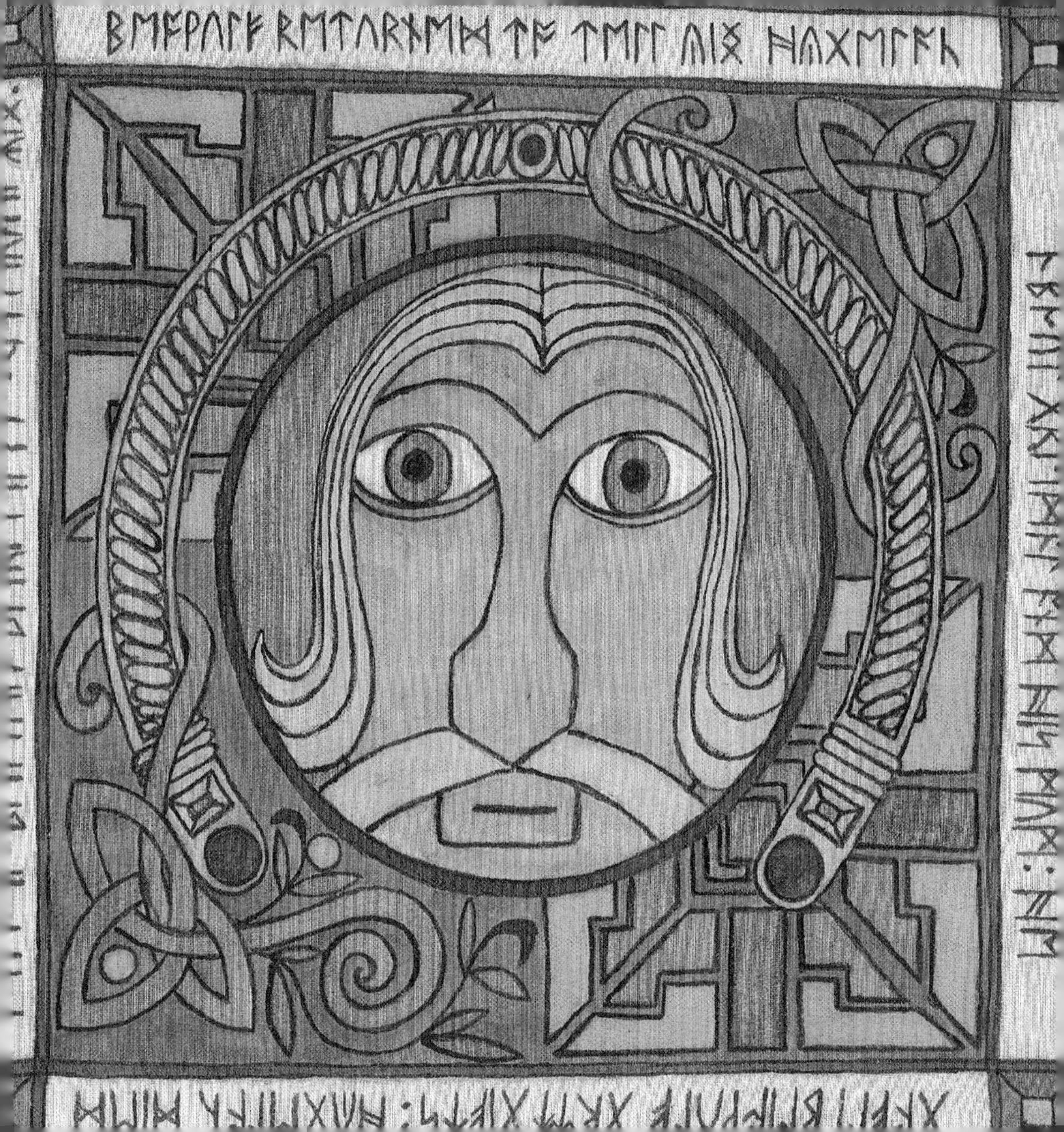

Fifty years later, a slave stole a goblet from a high roofed barrow, full of treasures, guarded by an immense dragon.

The theft awoke the scaly beast.

Angry, he went on the rampage breathing fire.

Homes and forts were burnt to dust, and King Beowulf, the hero, confronted the dragon, but his faithful sword, Naegling, let him down.

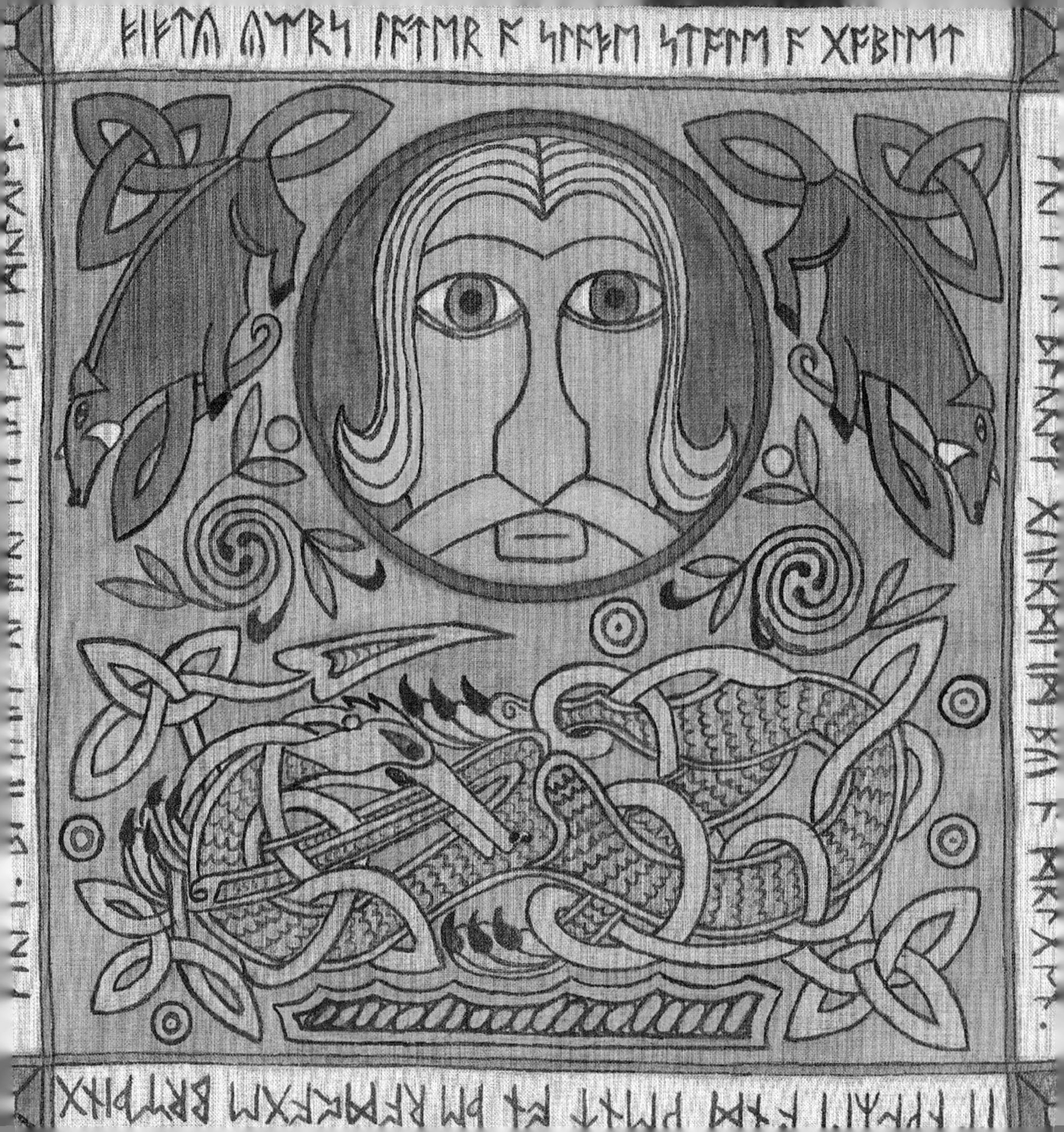

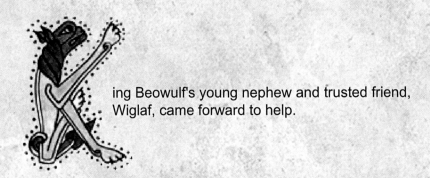 ing Beowulf's young nephew and trusted friend, Wiglaf, came forward to help.

Flames flew all around. Hiding behind Beowulf's shield, Wiglaf rammed his sword into the dragon's belly as the dragon bit hard into Beowulf''s shoulder.

Blood poured down the King's body. Poison swirled around inside him. Although wounded, the King thrust his stabbing knife deep into the dragon's heart.

The fiery monster took his last breath.

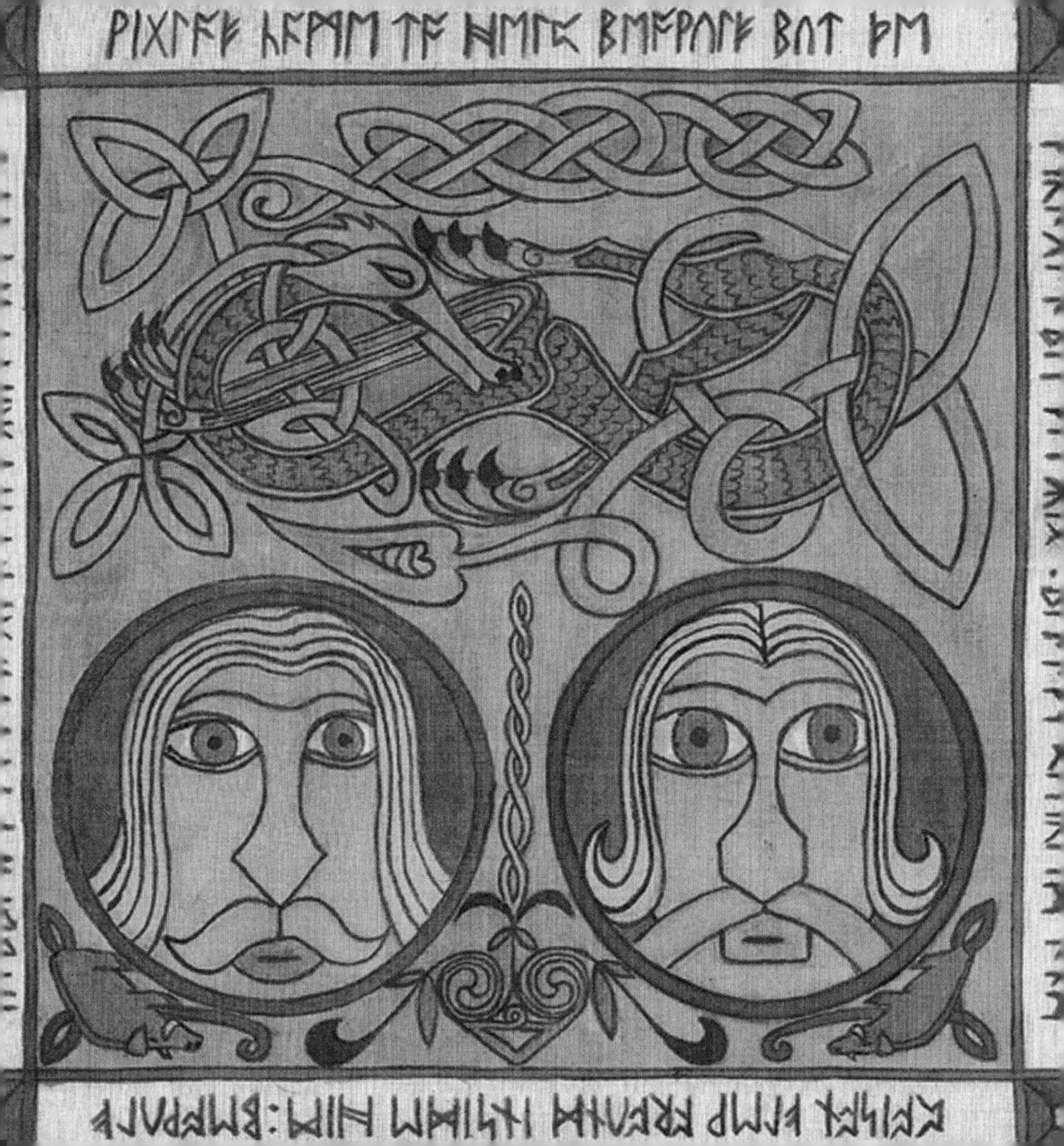

he brave warrior helped Beowulf, but it was no good, he was dying.

"I would like to take a look at some of the treasures before I go." whispered Beowulf weakly.

Wiglaf ran to the barrow and came back laden with golden bowls, plates and armbands. By the time the rest of the soldiers returned, after fleeing the rampaging dragon, they found their King dead.

 Iglaf announced, "We shall build a huge funeral pyre, hung with gold, helmets, shields and chainmail."

Women wailed as the body of King Beowulf burned.

Ten days later, a massive barrow was built, high on a cliff for all to see. Inside, King Beowulf's ashes were laid, along with his treasures.

King Beowulf, the hero, confronted the dragon.

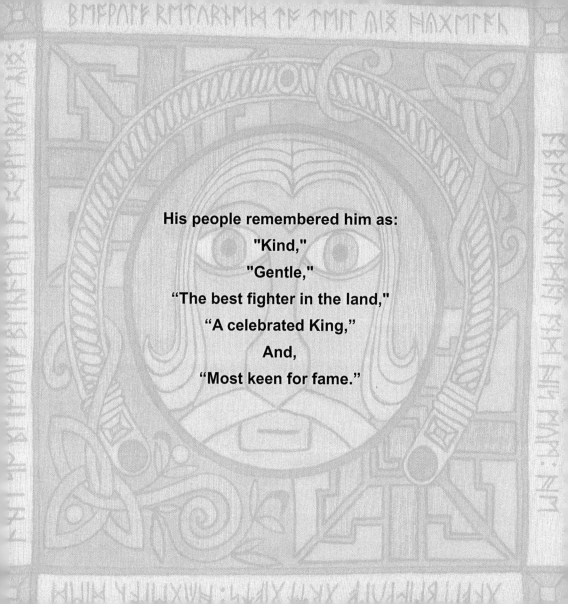

His people remembered him as:

"Kind,"

"Gentle,"

"The best fighter in the land,"

"A celebrated King,"

And,

"Most keen for fame."

Rune

Rune comes from the old Norse word 'runa' meaning a 'secret' or 'mystery'. The runes represent objects, gods, people, animals' concept and occurrences.

The Anglo-Saxons brought their own writing system when they invaded Britain. It is thought that the first alphabet started life amongst the Germanic tribes in northern Europe around 200AD and was known as Futhorc (after the first six runes). There are between 16 and 34 symbols, and there are variations in their form due to usage over the centuries.

I have used 28 symbols in my book; notice how similar some of the runes are to our modern alphabet.